this is not

by scarlett mabel

this is not a memoir

FIRST EDITION

to m,
"'cause i could live
by the light in
your eyes"
-sarah bareilles

this is not a memoir

~

scarlett mabel

what i had

this is not a memoir

~

so what is this?

this is not a memoir
this is not an ode
this is not a story
and this is not being told

these are just words
simply, sewn together
their meaning means less
than the weight of a feather

do not ask
where the words first thought
for i will have to say with greed
from the alphabet i bought

from the alphabet i bought
and paid for with sins
this is not a memoir
they are simply my skins

this is not a memoir

a mother's promise

mommy, mommy
i scraped my knee
i've never seen blood
what could this be

mommy, mommy
he pulled my hair
i cried at recess
and everyone stared

mommy, mommy
why are you going
i don't want to go
there, time is slowing

mommy, mommy
it's been some time
i'm all grown up
i even set my own bedtime

mommy, mommy
why didn't you stop her
for six years
you became a blur

mommy, mommy
it's my turn to leave
it's hurts less to know
you won't ever grieve

~mommy mommy, will i ever be enough?

her eyes

her eyes
were etched into my lids
they pierced my soul
and left me breathless
a memory ingrained
to which time is nothing

~why are you doing this to me?

to nana, i see you

i see you in the night sky
and when i brush my hair
the way i see my smile
a quality, i hope we'd share

i hear you in the roar
of the ocean and it's tide
the melody of the breeze
in the beauty it cannot hide

i feel you in the sun
and the warmth of a summer night
the embrace of a friend
and the depth of all my might

i see you in my dreams
and in the books i read at night
and when it gets too dark to see
i see you in the light

i hear you in the silence
and the pitter-patter of the rain
and deep into my sleep
the serenade of the midnight train

sometimes i don't know who to hate
when we never stood a chance
never got to see your face
not even for a glance

i see you in the moon
and when i wake, the morning dew
and when i speak to you before bed
i hope you see me too

rose

you may have been a rose
so beautiful and sweet
but you were covered in thorns
you watched me bleed

you can't take back
the words you fired at me
they left bullet holes
i'm on my knees

~a song i'll never write

this is not a memoir

my villain

you held my innocence in your palm
looked me straight in the eye
and crumbled it, as if it was nothing to begin with
what a lovely beginning

you broke my heart, before i learned to love
gave me darkness before i saw light
you broke me before i knew what being whole was like
drowned me before i learned to swim

because if you, i lost what i never had
you stole parts of me that i never experienced
my future became yours

took my blessings and locked them in a box
with a key, never to exist
to which i'd try to create my own
success never did come about

you blessed me with hate like no other
watched as my happiness turned to dust
and you blew it away
a poisonous grin etched on your face

my nights were filled with visions of you
and what would come of our next encounter
i would awake in puddles of tears and fear
knowing you are not far away

would your mother be proud
knowing her daughter had become a villain
to a girl that would never know she was a princess

~why would a kid ever write something like this?

this is not a memoir

you make me incomplete

you make me incomplete
with every aching heartbeat
and i can't put on my shoes
without the thought of you
damn, you make me incomplete

~another song i'll never finish

sign off

name here
here
and here
sign off your happiness
love, and mentality

pen and ink
became
knife and blood
this is your oath

you are too young
you don't know what's best
leave it to me
i've left the nest

goodbye life
goodbye love
see you someday
maybe, i don't know

sigh here
here
and here

this is not a memoir

will to survive

ratty hair
sore heart
stinging eyes
beating heart

closing the door
shutting the lights
counting her prayers
saying goodnight

gapped teeth
scars of old
pigtails
desire to be bold

scarlett mabel

you are my graffiti

streaks of red
blotches of yellow
turn to sand in my hands
your voice becomes mellow

a lullaby in your scream
a symphony in your cries
tell me again
i want to hear your lies

whip me with your words
scar with your eyes
look at me again
another promise dies

sing me to sleep
with the hymn of your breathing
my heart throbs in my chest
the scar of your beating

"why don't you run"
they ask again each time
i tell them, i am a clock
you, my chime

this is not a memoir

i wish i loved you

i wish i loved you
i wish i cared
i wish you meant more to me
if only you could compare

i wish i found beauty
in your eyes and soul
i wish i could fall in love
i wish i could make you whole

if i close my eyes
and think so so hard
i can almost picture it
it catches me off guard

where i love your laugh
and the way you dance
i don't hate your taste
or the size of your pants

i wish i loved you
and you know i try
everyday i look into the mirror
and try not to cry

~is there an age restriction on self-hate?

scarlett mabel

fairy bed sheets

i was raised in emptiness
a single breath
a soldem torch
and fairy bed sheets

i was raised on the edge of language
cracked windows
dead houseplants
and lemon

i was taught math
as i ran from the time
for me it did not exist

what was the future
if nothing ever changed
would i ever change
these fairy bed sheets

surrounded

what does one call noise
that does not contain the innocence to be white
untroubled it is not
it suffocates me

i sit here, amongst unknown
it asks if I would like to join
flashes their enchanting grin
i smile and excuse myself
for i am not one for enchantment

symmetrical beings
slight off copies
nothing circles their thoughts
but one another
i can't
i can't

the whirlpool of waves
turns my vision
i'm seeing through water
clouds of turbulence
so the only occupant left
is famine for the mind

the steady hum of my atmosphere
engross my every cell
they are I
but I am not them

~fostered by a world of fake smiles and~

when it gets bad

when it gets bad
snow in my head
ache in my chest
the fire i used to feel so deeply
gone

when it gets bad
i never wake
dreams cloak reality
wake up
wake up
wake up

when it gets bad
i stop writing
stop reading
stop singing
stop

~my life is a red light

scarlett mabel

i cannot write about people

i can not write about people
for their behavior i do not understand
but bestow upon me a pen
and i shall paint my sorrow till end

where i am from

birthed through rubble
i sit on a throne
it isn't much to see
but i can call it my own

i stride on wavelengths
burrow in words
hide from plain sight
just to be heard

from music and novels
the words intertwine
to create a masterpiece
that lives in my mind

the blood in my vessels
pump to the beat
the marching of an army
the stomp of their feet

my guardian angel
sits in the clouds
sets her eyes upon me
a mere face in the crowds

"why," she says,
"do you wish so hard?"
i tell her
"the best words come,
from those who are scarred"

the best words come
from those who are scared
then call me shakespeare
and maybe it won't be so hard

~at least he was remembered for his pain~

hello?

when i look in my mirror
there's a man staring back
i nod my head down
i don't look like that

he has great big ears
and a large yellow hat
that conceals his face
his eyes of a cat

how to be present

the crushing
the burning
the cracks in my head

the fire
the sea
let me go to bed

being awake is going to war
don't ask me mother
i'm much too sore

stay awake
for the world and it's silence
but the sun is my signal
she is my guidance

the burning continues
but i can't feel it now
i want to be here
i just don't know how

the new girl

cripple me silly
and sing me to sleep
release craves my body
my body, it can keep

my legs are numb
and my heart decays
the mind is down
temporary delays

words mean nothing
when your eyes are shut
the world, supposedly a shelter
and me, the mutt

kill them and cry
as their mothers always do
and flock someone new
like a sinner in a pew

(nothing can be a clean slate anymore)

paint me red

paint me red
scar your cheeks
scream my name
for the wind to hear

black and blue
a tear or two
blurry eyes
and muffled cries

tell them why
and they shall follow
lead the way
my words, i swallow

no longer my life
no longer my will
you are they predator
and i, your last kill

anger is the blood

anger is the blood
and wounds are trauma
there's red
there's red
there's red

crawl
stand
fall
shake

kiss me goodnight
before you go
so in the morning
the emptiness
will feel more real

self destruction

kick me
punch me
turn me red

watch as i drank
the sea in bed

drowning
save me
if you try
what is left?
to say goodbye

this is self destruction

autism

i crave words
like a cigarette between my fingers
the heat of its flame
the mercy of its smoke

they give it a funny name
with three funny syllables
but i just call it me
what else should it be?

they say it's my obsession
I say it's just some fun
they tell me i need help
maybe they're sick one

what can they do
when there is no label
to slap on you?

a girl thing

she had lust on her finger tips
and fire in her throat
how i longed to be
the topic of the songs she wrote

~google: what to do if you think a girl is pretty?

i hurt myself

i hurt myself
with fabric not made for me
and songs to which i do not sing along
the sea of bodies i do not know
have become more me than
my own "hello"

i hurt myself
with the figures to which surround
the exams i cram
and writing which does not give me joy

i hurt myself
for so long
and so much
because i thought it would hurt more
just to be me

~definition: me
who?

how i imagined us

july
the sun lightenes my hair
and darkens your skin
the freckles on my face
have swallowed my nose

our skin is warm
and there's sand in our hair
we laugh because
july may end
but we are eternal

~for this was the good

go fish

i told him about the fence
and the arched doorways
i told him about the garden
and the water just outside

i told him about italy
the fruits and olives
i told him about my life
the one i want to live

"go fish"

the first time

the first time a boy
told me he loved me
i told him i loved
the rain
and little did i know
that was the beginning
of the great and undeniable
push

~L, we both weren't ready

this is not a memoir

i remember

i remember your smile
when i caught you stare
and when you'd say how
god had finally answered your prayer

i remember the way your hands
would engulf my stubby fingers
the touch you left on my body
to this day, still lingers

i remember the way you listened
to the stubbornness of my words
and when you didn't know what to say
we'd stop, and listen to the birds
(they fought in song)

i remember the day you'd say
that she had your heart instead
i wish i had stolen it
and kept it warm in my bed

and when she broke it too
i remember the way you cried
and told me i was the one
and how it hurt to say goodbye

scarlett mabel

an abundance of salt

it's hard to see
the amount of salt
in the ocean
until the water is gone

for me,
i didn't see how much
of you i hated
until you left

because the hate stayed
because you left me
because you loved her

the salt didn't leave
with the water this time

(and you said it would
never happen again)

ault ault

leave him

if he says
that you're too good
paints himself
in colors of the sea
leave him

if he calls
to say he's scared
that your friends are too close
and he wants you more
leave him

if he touches you
in red and blue
and cries for them
and promises it's the end
leave him

he might be good
most of the time
but, darling, he's not

pack your things
and cry of his absence
don't let his promises
cloak his ways
leave him

~never let love strangle you~

paradox

broken glass
wildflowers
a bitter drink
a few more hours

call me a paradox
call me a sin
call me what you want
you'll still never win

walk away
run, if you must
but don't call me yours
in that, you can trust

scarlett mabel

love, ocean

when you crave a love
to reach the depths of all oceans,
you can't expect to swim
you can only drown
how is the real issue
to drown and stay afloat

so many words

i write many words
for someone who does not feel
who does not cry
it almost seems unreal

i don't remember the last time
my eyes stung with emotion
my heart so cold
i call her the atlantic ocean

i call her the atlantic ocean
for the harshness of her breath
and because when most come close
they are met with their death

scarlett mabel

my words

my words have become less and less
once burning the pages
they have hit a dam
with no way to break

my words mean less and less
to me, to you, to reality

what a bitch
my stanzas have become
no longer the ordered pairs
stacked upon each other
lines of four
they hit the floor

my words have become less and less mine
as if an imposter has stolen my hands
and written

the words mean nothing
except to myself
so if you're reading this
and trying to relate a feeling
i'm sorry
you can't

if you want to be loved

if you want to be loved
take a step out the door
your foolishness adornes me
you are pure to the core

tell me again
about your soul shearing day
of when mommy and daddy
decided not to stay

now it's my turn
although i could not compare
just a little girl like me
i could never dare

it started out like any other
as i started my trek
the dark side approaches
i could already feel
their fingers around my neck

scarlett mabel

~

this is not a memoir

what you gave me

scarlett mabel

~

your eyes are blue

your eyes are blue
and that itself
tends to be metaphorical

my eyes are hazel
two colors merged to one
and neither
are the same as yours

you ask my favorite color
and for the longest time i didn't know
"i like them all" i'd say
but now i know

it was oblivious to me
even when i dyed my hair
and painted my walls
i matched my sheets
and colored my nails

there are two colors in my eyes
and one in yours
but when I became my own destruction
you, my love, became salvation
and so did your stupid blue eyes

broken window

a broken window
a solemn stone
two swam together
just for today

i find it funny
how this could end
and yet, you defy

i am glass
and you a stone

you could if you wanted to, ya know?
destroy me?

if i was your juliet

in the midst of bonds, friendship was gold and love
was a forest fire
unforgivable by any means
but their flame was concealed from eyes of peril
only fed by swift moments of their longing souls

staying unseen was the chore of aching hearts
throbbing with every unseen glance
hiding their lustful skin was porcelain faces of typical
lives
their hearts trembling with secreted passion

remaining in classes of numbers and honored persons
hardly able to stay fixed, a more powerful force
present
their bodies had been replaced with magnets
and opposites they were

lost time accumulates and oftentimes so would
sleepless nights
their words held more persuasion than a million coffee
beans
oh but to the sunset they could run, away from all
forests of tinder
where their flame could flourish to their heart's
content

to be their own fairytale, another for the books
cinderella and her prince would sit in envy
jealous of a disastrous love?
or to be part of something so capable

~we could do it, you know?

storybound

who was rhett before scarlett?
who was bonnie before clyde?
was there a romeo before juliet?
did any exist before the collide?

what im saying
although not very clear
is that im still here
the before
im here

because we,
are simply
storybound

scarlett mabel

piano

play me like a piano
a melody so sweet
and suddenly i've fallen
no longer incomplete

hold me through the night
and be there when i wake
let's talk about life
the one we'd like to make

~yet another song i'll never finish

until you came around

how should i write
too young and too in love
to not know
what either mean?

what do i do with this
what do i do?

i knew what i wanted
knew where to go
i was ready for my fate
and then you

saved me?
if you'd call it that

(how do you save someone from their own destiny?)

scarlett mabel

ode to thee

as I gaze into thee
the ocean roars
calm but chaotic
soft but fierce

the whole sky is condensed
into two pearls upon thy face
my afternoon blue
and midnight constellations

knife to her throat
blinding light in the dark
"put down your weapons"
the silent poet spoke

who knew such small stones
could break down her walls
windows to the soul
crystals of infinity
my ode to thee

the type

maybe you aren't the type that everyone writes their
love poems about
but you were mine

and in the end, i'll be sorry
so i say it now

thank you

do it all

i could write a million metaphors
for the way your eyes look up close
or the softness of your voice

i could sing to you every love song
and mean every word
and still have more to say

i could spend my whole life
proving to you
your own beauty and elegance

i'll take you to mystical lands
and explore places and their people
we'd forget that melancholy ache
that we used to hold so dear

but none of it matters
because you forgot about me
and i don't think i will

have you seen

you once told me in a dream
that you have never seen the ocean
i laughed
"how silly", i said
"you look in the mirror every morning,
don't you?"

scarlett mabel

if i could count

if i could count the ways you can make me feel
maybe i wouldn't be here
writing a million lines
in hopes that you feel one

this is not a memoir

tell me a story

tell me a story
but beginnings are clique
so think for me dear

page one is boring
i want to know what went into
the first word
think, we have time

when was the first time
you knew
when did you become aware

take my hand

baby,
take my hand
and lead me
to where i
would never go
and maybe
just maybe
we'll go
crazy
together

golden boy

eyes of ocean
smile of sun
you are on my mind on a constant run

i ask and i ask
and i know it's unfair
but give me something
no, nothing at all

tears to streams
ache to shatter
my heart was the ball
and you, the batter

once the golden boy
now lives on
as a meaningless coy
(or so i tell myself)

scarlett mabel

tell me you love me

tell me you love me
or say that you don't
i'm looking for answers
but don't say that you don't

the things that i feel
it can't just be me
tell me you love me
or that we could be

~another song that i'll never write

monsters

when a monster is bad
nobody questiones it
why would they?
if they were only doing
what they were meant to do

i don't remember the day
you became a monster
i must have decided that
someone like you
couldn't be someone like me

i don't remember when you turned from my salvation
to devastation

because it's you

because i wish for you
in every four leafed clover
every shooting star
every 11:11

and in every love poem
i picture us

you fill my mind
and break my heart
but when i look at you
i only see art

you are my dream
my wish and my plea
but you are not my reality

i'm not there to make you laugh
or hold you when you cry
i'm not the person you go to for help
but sometimes in my head i lie

i dream and i dream
and when i wake, some more
im sorry i've done this
and i'm sorry it had to be you

if only

if only if only
what i wrote were true
i'd see you here
i wish i do

if only if only
you'd take my hand
and run away
run away

if only if only
i was someone new
someone you'd risk
and say "i do"

if only if only
i'd let this go
and stop writing about a boy
whom i'll never know

~i'm sorry, and yet i still write?

hate is a strong word

i hate myself
because i still love you
because i'm sorry
because i'm not done

i hate myself
because i know
how it is to be wanted
by someone we don't

but i also hate you
for making me feel
this.

how dare you

how dare you
come into my life
change my world
and walk away

how dare you
ask me to stay
and not be there
when i do

I breathe now
because you asked
but sometimes i wish
I knew

I wish i knew
that you'd be gone
and my will go too
would force its way
down my throat
until i almost do

but i don't
because your stupid blue eyes
keep me awake
how dare you

scarlett mabel

can you tell

can you tell
that the way i look at you
differs completely
to the way you look at me

can you tell
when i've had a dream
of us and it all
and wake up to nothing

where i get lost in unconsciousness
where you and i
become the we i have always longed

can you tell
how much it hurts
to see you so happy
and to be embarrassed
at my own jealousy?

can you tell?
do you ever notice?

~it's funny how
my whole mental world is you
and you can't even tell~

why don't you care

~i did not like the beginning, and it felt foolish to rewrite, here is where i offer myself~

but you don't answer
you leave me here
writing like you care
and hoping i'm all wrong

please, i'll beg
if that'll make you come
but you won't see this either
and if you did
you couldn't recognize
me

~i wrote a whole book about this boy hoping that he'd read maybe one word. knowing that he won't. why would he? he doesn't even know me. so to whoever may be reading this, thank you, and please just let them know how you feel. this life is not eternal, and if you never tell them, you'll never know. let it be known. there will come a day where you regret your silence~

selfish

i know i'm selfish
i know it's bad
i know my existence
makes you mad

let me say
as straightforward as i can
i know i'm too much for you
but it's okay
its mutual

i push and i pull
and ask you to stay
then i walk straight out
no feelings at bay

i cry at night
and write poetry into the stars
i tell them all about you
and sing them a few bars

what they don't know
is that we've barely ever met
and i think it's quite funny
but i'm not stopping yet

this is not a memoir

salt/na/sodium

the ocean
my tears
a family dinner
they cheer

the winter
the ice
the roads
think twice

too much
and one could die
too little
and goodbye

the ocean
my tears
you're everywhere
my dear
Na

candy

you were the candy
that i could never
put down

and i didn't wash my mouth
because i knew
even a cavity
was better than
leaving nothing behind

~a taste doesn't last forever~

little words

little words
like
pitter
patter
grace the street
look at my feet
where they have been
where they will go
i'm scared to know
if i'll see you
happy with someone new
i'll sit in a pew
and pray to a God
that i don't believe in
i'll ask him for you
even if
it's the last thing
i deserve

scarlett mabel

~

this is not a memoir

what is left

scarlett mabel

this is not a memoir

tequila

i told him i was tequila
and he didn't know what i meant
"you're so silly, el,
i never know."

i told him i was tequila
because i'm bitter and sad
and because i'm no good
unless i'm disguised

in the morning he'll know
when he feels lost and confused
and someone will be there
with a glass of water

there's always someone for them
to be there once i go
because i'm just tequila
and after, a headache

scarlett mabel

silence

silence knocked on my door
i let them in and sat down for a cup of coffee

we laid in bed
and did nothing all day

we went for a walk
and smiled at strangers

when it was time for them to go
i understood and opened the door

the first time i spoke
my voice was raspy
and unrecognizable
but i knew
it was time

raven

who will comfort the raven while she weeps?
for the hell in her mind
and her crippled wings
no longer carry her to tomorrow

who will give empathy
to the symbol of destruction
when her days are long
and nights so endless

does she not deserve
a kind mind
to lay side by side while her world is on fire?

she'll give you stories
and wipe a tear
she'll ask you how
you live a year

who will comfort the raven while she weeps?
born into a metaphorical world
there is nothing left
she slips into the netherworld

scarlett mabel

what a coincidence

what a coincidence
was what i said
as i noticed that his eyes resembled
the pearls in your head

what a coincidence
that his hair
fell like i had once seen
on your skin, so fair

was it the way he looked at me
and i immediately saw you
or was it that i wanted you
to look at me like he did

for i was a psychic
and you, my crystal ball
and when you didn't come
it was he, who i call
what a coincidence

too much

she told me that in love
she craved the moon
that the stars were tokens
and the sun a promise

she said her goal
was to make the night sky jealous
and to wear it's jewels
as a noose

this only dampened
and did not absorb
until she said the most important thing
slam the door

she said
"i crave a love
that is too
much"

scarlett mabel

can't imagine

hi i'm scarlett
we may have met
oh, you have to leave
but i'm not ready yet

you may not know me
you probably don't remember
but there's more here
than you can see

see, my name isn't actually scarlett
and you do know my name
but the rest i don't know
and that is a shame

oh, yeah
why am i here?
to tell you goodbye
while i stay here

see m,
the truth is
i can't imagine
living in small town wherever
without you here

and i know it's selfish
i know i'm mad
but you were the greatest love
that i've never had

and the city will love you
the lights will shine
correct me if i
have crossed a line

its sad and it's sweet
and clique and boring
but i ask if you
could remember

just every once in a while
remember

i can't imagine this town
without knowing
that you're a part of it

(but that's something i'll have to get over, isn't it?)

scarlett mabel

timeline

i made a timeline
to where i could see you in the future

it started just to remember
that you could remember
me

from graduations
to concerts
i'll never miss

because saying goodbye
seems like so much less
when i know i'll see you again

it's easier to know that
a "next time" is out there
i'll see you then

tell me a story

"tell me a story"

there once was a girl
who tripped over her own feet
wore princess dresses everywhere
and fought deep within

there once was a boy
wore innocence as a mask
with his big sky eyes
and hands of bandages

now you can imagine
the world and their ways
pushing them together
like physics and magnets

now imagine Shakespeare
sitting, quill in hand
writing the tragedy
of the two bound hearts

in years to come
everyone would read
about him and I
and how we never became we

years

it's been years
and months
and weeks
and days

from 11 and hungry
to 16 and chaotic
i never forgot
i never forgot

forgive me now
for i have sinned
years without your touch
and the earth's atmosphere has thinned

is it too late?
to ask you now
the burning question of my adolescence
would you allow?

am i enough?
are you proud?

this is not a memoir

only me

my knuckles painted with ash
the grip they hold has surpassed its lifetime
but the pain doesn't transcend the fear
for a world where there is no you and I

they long for your presence
of you beyond my prolonged grasp
the world awaits

you are what keeps me going
going where, I don't know
i am to weak to move
but with you I am not alone

my body does not listen
when I say it's time to set you free
It has a mind of its own
and a soul so broken and weary

my grip never hesitates
because if you could soar
i know I couldn't follow
my strength doesn't add up well
for it was drained a while back

scarlett mabel

i know that letting you go
would destroy me
but keeping you here
is so so cruel

i am the restraint
prisoning you into me
you are the balloon
not my key

i soon give up and let you free
my cheeks who were once burdened with drought
wow are moistened by my eyes
i search but there is no key

(you would have gone anyway)

reality

she sank,
"darling there is rain"
the floor is wet
and my feet slip

she falls,
"honey there is pain"
an ache, if you will
it's suffocating

I lay too
and ask her
"would you like to share?"

~save me, reality~

should i resent you

should i resent you
for the fire you never gave?
for the passion i never saw
for what i crave

i don't
and that's the short answer
i don't

you weren't a wildfire
or a midnight thunderstorm
you never tore down my world
in the way of such an art form

but you were my morning shower
cleansing me for the day
you were the warm water
and for that i pray

although you never made me question
what the hell you were there for
you spoke to me like an old book
and an old book, i adore

~L, again

raven ii

the raven weeps, eyes of sorrow, mind of pain
she cries for the unloved, the heartbroken, and the
oblivious
she cries for her mother, whom life took too much
and her father, who could never give the love he
should have
the raven weeps for the other who walked away
the one who never gave the girl a chance
maybe he was scared, maybe just too young
or maybe he had his reasons, but neither could cover
his destruction
the raven cries for the girl, who life played like a deck
of cards
and very rarely gave her a good hand
she cried seeing her heartbreak, time after time
when she thought the boy would come back, but broke
every time he didn't
for she was the unloved, the heartbroken, and maybe
the most oblivious of all
she weeps for them all, but what does that do?
for maybe the one she weeps for the most,
is you

sirius

the star outside my window
who watches me while i sleep
is named after my first love
he watches me while i weep

the star outside my window
sees me nearly a decade ago
and as i wave and say hello
i watch him as he glow

the star outside my window
whom i share many secrets
lives so very far away
in the universe and it's deepness

(am i crazy sirius, am i out of my mind? Now we must
wait fourteen years for a response)

this is not a memoir

i hope

i hope my soul
bounces around time
like it means nothing

i hope my soul
has seen the creation and destruction
of this world we call home

i hope my soul
has meet people i read about in school
and ones that will read about me
(maybe they know me)

i wonder if i read my own words
in another life, both knowing and unsure why i feel
them so deeply

for souls are not bound to time like the bodies to who
they are tied
they jump forward and back
the "future" simply does not exist

~why must time exist here~

scarlett mabel

so I can learn

today i took some pictures
and i took them for me
to tell myself
that i am pretty
in nothing but my own skin

i didn't brush my hair
or powder my face
i didn't smile or laugh
i was naked in every way

there are a million things
society will tell me are unpretty

starting with the dark circles behind my eyes
and the scars on my face
to my uneven shoulders
and the curve of my nose

now i took this pictures
and stare at them everyday
because i'm teaching myself
that beauty is not what i am
but who

and so i sat against a blank wall
and took black and white photos
of nothing but my skin
and everytime i think i am unpretty
i say "fuck them, i don't have to be"

life is the lesson

i'm learning me
and who i am
who i want to be
and where

i'm learning who will be there
and who will leave
i'm learning how much i want to show
and what to keep

it's hard to love
with a broken heart
and i know it's clique
but some good things are

this is not a memoir

when the sky weeps

the sky cries
and weeps onto my shoulders
and the weight of the world
drowns my clothes

i'll stay
and wait out the storm
because i know
how it feels
to fall apart

then the sun will come
and i'll go inside
and let the tears of the sky
dry on my skin

hurt will always hurt
and you must be able
to let it be felt
but it shall pass
and absorb into your skin

~there is no pain
worth not being felt~

Renowned question

one thing you must ask yourself is
"do you want more people to visit your grave
or bow at your throne"

epilogue

this is me, walking away from you

i may never know how you reciprocate

but it is unfair to pursue an idea that is immaterial

may we meet again,

you know who i am

Printed in Great Britain
by Amazon

30870787R00061